Breezi's Island

By Jeanne Buesser

Books by Jeanne Buesser

Her websites are:
www.jeannebuesser.com
www.apraxianetwork.org

Additional books she has written are:
Water Line
Willow Tree
He Talks Funny

Her poetry books include:
Moonlight Till Dawn
Journey From Darkness To Light

Look for upcoming books:
Toxchi's Journey
Wuffle's Adventure
Caramel's Meadow

Acknowledgments

I would like to thank my parents, for the wonderful opportunity to live in Kenya, East Africa, during my childhood years.

I have been inspired to live and write from my heart by my sweet friend M.

Editing my book with Andrea and DC was fun and inspiring because it helped me think outside the box. Thank you for your help.

Thank you Alphagraphics for your help with the layout and cover for my book.

Thank you to my sisters for taking the time to read through my book and offer their wise suggestions. Also to June, my fellow author, thanks for her tips and review and support.

I am always grateful for all the seen and unseen support and inspiration I receive for my creativity.

Introduction

As a stay-at-home mom, Jeanne Buesser founded the non-profit Apraxia Network and became a sought-after speaker and author on the neurological speech disorder called Apraxia. She developed her poetry and art and began publishing at the age of 49. She and her two sons live in New Jersey.

Chapter 1

Breezi

Breezi grew up in a village surrounded by mountains, where papaya, banana, and mango trees flourished in the rich, red soil of Kenya. While her family managed a grocery business, young Breezi turned instead to raising crops. She observed how they grew, learned to plant and water the seeds and helped pick the crops when they were ripe.

Maize and beans constituted the predominant crops. Villagers brought their crops to the market where Breezi would engage in lively conversation and learn more about the local lore and history.

The young woman grew to be a bright and energetic girl with shoulder length wavy hair with auburn highlights. Inquisitive dark eyes complemented Breezi's willing smile. She truly loved life itself and the people in her life.

Often Breezi would reflect on her unusual background, and would question how her English mother had found her way to a small village in the East African country. Her mother, Sara, would explain, "My family originated in England. There was an opportunity to expand their grocery business into Kenya so I moved to Kenya as a young child and learned all about the dry goods business as I grew up."

She continued, "When I met your father at university and we discovered our mutual interests, we chose to move back to his village in order to provide services and products that the town had never had."

Breezi asked Sara, "Mum, how did you choose my name?" Her mother replied, "While pregnant with you, never once did I become sick. Easy labor followed and you continue now to act as an easy child. To cap things off, a very breezy windstorm prevailed on the day of your birth."

Breezi's teachers encouraged her to pursue a university education. She would need to find a job and move far away from her parents. Breezi approached her parents to present her plan, since the university was a great distance from the family home. She explained this to her parents and aware of the sadness this may cause, Breezi promised to visit often and to always update them on her progress as a student.

Moving forward on her plan, she submitted an

application for university, excited by the possibilities offered by different classes. The process went quickly. Breezi's acceptance soon followed. From many years of saving the money earned from the sale of the crops she grew, Breezi had more than sufficient money to begin her life as a university student.

Breezi's parents reached out to a business customer who had a relative living in the city and stood ready to help Breezi's travel arrangements. How happy and grateful Breezi felt receiving the invitation to stay overnight there.

Chapter 2

Breezi's Departure

The day for Breezi's departure arrived. Breezi packed all her belongings and started her long journey. She found a ride into town and caught a local bus. Despite a bumpy ride, Breezi slept on the bus. She arrived late at her destination.

Early the next morning she reached the university

and signed up for classes. Breezi had always been a quick learner and one who enjoyed her studies. Looking back on her parents' success with the grocery store, marketing seemed both a reasonable and likely choice of a major.

Learning she would start classes soon, next on Breezi's agenda was finding a suitable place to live. At the local library she was able to find a room rental posted on the bulletin board. The new place was bright and cheery, and Breezi really enjoyed connecting with her new roommate, Timi.

She took a job in marketing to help offset her expenses. Her office was close by enabling an easy walk to work. Information gained in her night classes supported her new daytime job.

Chapter 3

Breezi's Friend Timi

Breezi's apartment was near a park where many dogs played with their owners. There was a small grassy area to sit down where a few trees provided shade.

She saved enough money from the job to buy a used laptop, enabling her to do some work at home when she had extra work. Learning to balance her work

with part-time college courses was an ongoing
challenge.

After several months she made friends with a few
of her co-worker's. Breezi was surprised at how
quickly she became successful at acquiring new
clients in the business world,especially considering
this was foreign territory for her.

Breezi's roommate, Timi, worked in the same field.
She had long auburn hair and green eyes. Timi had
worked at the job for a few years before Breezi, so
Timi showed her the ropes.

Together they worked very hard for long hours,
but time seemed to slip away, as Breezi became
proficient at her job. Months turned into years
while Breezi studied at nights. She then graduated.

Breezi's life included socializing with Timi. They
went out and enjoyed what city life had to offer. She
and Timi liked to go dancing and they ate at the local
hang-outs when they could.

Very late one evening, Breezi felt lonely. She
couldn't sleep and felt she needed to hear her
mother's voice. She phoned her mother.
"Mum, it's Breezi, I have a question to ask you.

How did you know that Father was the one for you?"

Sara took a long breath and told Breezi the romantic story.

"I attended college in Kenya. I met your father at the university where he studied business. John had grown up in a small village. He wanted to stretch his wings and learn more about the outside world. His family never went to college. It was up to him to expand on earning a living, finding a job and learning how to fend for himself - how to be able to go back and teach others in his community to manage their money.

"In my first class, sitting next to me was an African man with kind eyes and broad shoulders and a nice physique, and once he spoke I discovered his happy outlook on life." Sara continued, "Later, John told me he had to stop himself from staring at me for he, too, was powerfully attracted!"

Sara sighed. "Honestly, it was love at first sight for both of us.

"We were married soon after and founded our family dry goods business in a local village where he came from. The rest is history."

Breezi calmed down as she listened to her mother explain the mysteries of how two strangers came together in a beautiful and loving way.

She had never been in love before and didn't know what it felt like. She often wondered if there was a partner in her future, but was concerned because her job kept her too busy.

Meanwhile, Timi was looking forward to her future vacation. Timi received a ten day vacation bonus that included a free flight anywhere from the city where she worked. She had already saved up enough money for her own vacation. Knowing how hard Breezi had worked throughout college, she graciously considered gifting Breezi with the vacation package.

Breezi was very surprised and delighted to get this gift of friendship from Timi. Tears formed in her eyes, she was desperate to get away and felt extremely grateful.

"Thank you so much Timi," she exclaimed.

She had been preparing to travel for a long time, and was open to travel anywhere. In anticipation, she had already procured a passport. The first thing she did was open her laptop and start researching the best vacation place.

She wanted to be at a quieter place where there weren't a lot of tourists. Taking a few lessons to learn something new would be interesting.

Breezi was excited for the possibilities. She closed her eyes after looking at a few islands on the computer, circled her index finger and pointed to one. She opened her eyes and immediately called the travel agency to ask about this particular island. Where were the best places to stay and how much would they cost?

Breezi picked a hotel which had some bungalows on the beach and booked it along with her flight.

The weeks flew by and she had to think about what to pack. Toiletries, hat, clothes, bathing suit, money, passport, tickets. She was so excited, her stomach was in a knot. She packed everything into her suitcase and slammed down the top.

Breezi called the taxi that night. Because the departure time was early the next morning, tossing and turning all night resulted in little sleep. Her alarm went off. Before she knew it, the taxi driver was beeping his horn. The taxi sped to the airport.

Breezi glanced at the departure board to find the correct gate. She stumbled to the gate and waited for the departure time announcement. Her eyes were heavy from lack of sleep. Walking down the ramp to the plane, she hoped she would be able to sleep on the flight.

As Breezi trudged down the aisle towards her assigned seat, she glanced at a young man with blonde hair and blue eyes sitting among the other passengers. "Hmmm," she thought, "What a cute guy!" As she settled in, sleep overtook her and her dreams were elsewhere.

Chapter 4

Sande

Breezi had a great rest. The next thing she knew the plane was landing on the airstrip. She awoke with a start, after hearing the tires squealing on the tarmac. With the plane stopped, she took her bag in hand and briskly walked off the plane.

At the airport, the hotel had a shuttle service to pick her up. "How nice," she thought. The shuttle windows were open, the weather was warm, but not too hot. Looking outside Breezi delighted in seeing the aqua blue sky that was peaceful and relaxing. Local birds flew by. She watched the wild green scenery on the side of the road. The shuttle bus drove a long time on the road from the airport. In the distance a large hotel appeared. It was beautifully landscaped.

As they drove up a long circular driveway covered in white gravel pebbles, she saw a gigantic pond with swans and ducks floating in its water. She wondered out loud, "How long has this hotel been here?" she asked the driver. He replied, "Over 100 years, Ma'am. The original settlers came here from Europe."

The entrance was made of white stone blocks in the form of a curved structure, with large columns and palm trees on either side. Awnings covered the large windows. A thatched roof seemed like it was a sight to behold. Breezi immediately loved this place - its simplicity, its beauty.

Breezi bent down so she didn't hit her head on the low door and walked out with her bag towards the front desk. The lobby and furnishings featured earthy tones.

"Welcome to the Sandz Hotel, Ma'am," said the doorman. "Did you have a good flight?"

"Yes, thank you," replied Breezi.

Arriving at the reception desk, she was asked, "May I see your reservation please?" Breezi handed him the paperwork. The clerk glancing down, and seemed confused after reading it.

"Oh dear, I'm so sorry. There must have been an overbooking on your bungalow. It isn't available at this time," the desk clerk said glancing at the computer screen.

"What am I going to do now?" a distressed Breezi

cried, sitting down hard, feeling at a loss.

"Ma'am, I do have another bungalow available which is at a lower price because it's a little smaller. It is a longer walk."

"Fine, I'll take that one then," Breezi agreed.

"Thank you for your patience and sorry for the inconvenience. Enjoy your stay in bungalow 36." He handed her the keys, a map to her bungalow and a receipt. "Please call us if you have any problems, just dial 0." He turned to help the next customer.

Luggage in hand, Breezi had a hard time locating the path to her bungalow. A small pathway wound around the hotel, with a few scattered signs with arrows attached to wooden posts in the ground. Warm breezes swayed the trees along the way.

The road wasn't properly kept, the bushes were overgrown. The trees were larger, with big palm branches, coconut clusters loomed high under their leaves. She wasn't sure how safe it was, they seemed heavy with the weight.

Breezi saw the bungalow in the distance. She came across a small, crooked, faded sign with a series of bungalow numbers pointing in either direction.

The path wasn't well maintained. Her bungalow appeared with branches partially blocking the doorway. The shutters were hung loosely outside the windows. She glanced up noticing that the thatched roof needed some fixing. Some of the fronds were missing. She thought she saw a small hole.

It had been a long walk and she was tired. Sighing, pushing aside the branches near the door, she put the key in the lock clicking it. The door creaked as she slowly pushed it open.

On Breezi's right was a tidy stocked kitchen, with a small table and chairs. She noticed a door opening in front of her that led up to a small sitting area and a bedroom with a phone and window."This is pretty nice," she spoke out loud. Fans in the ceilings brought a breeze into the rooms. Sunshine beamed through a glass window, bringing light into the room.

The walls were painted pale blue with patterned curtains on the windows. A bathroom was on her left and a multi-flowered curtain was hiding a sliding door down the hall. She unpacked her suitcase.

After a while it became dark and she longed for company while sitting in her room. Breezi stood up and remembered the hotel activities that were listed on the bulletin board in the lobby. One of the activities was dancing at the lounge with live music.

It occurred to her that she could eat dinner at the lounge and dance afterwards.

She wondered what outfit she should wear to the

lounge. She began to look through the dresser. Excited now, she began dressing. Maybe she would meet someone, Breezi mused.

Wearing a simple, sexy black dress, Breezi walked down the path to the hotel. Breezi studied the dinner menu. The lounge was very nicely decorated and soft music was playing, but there were few single people there and Breezi felt even more alone. Many dancing on the floor were couples. Breezi ate dinner and then stayed as long as she could, hoping someone would show up who was also alone.

The long day was catching up with her and Breezi headed back to her remote bungalow, thinking, "I will call the front desk to clear the pathway and repair the roof when I get back to my room."

Even though it was late, she picked up the phone near her bed. "Front desk, may I help you?" answered the person on duty.

She listed the tree limbs that needed removal that were blocking her door. She wanted the shutters tightened. The front door squeaked and needed oiling.

"We will send someone to your bungalow tomorrow, thank you for calling, good night," the front desk clerk stated before hanging up.

Breezi went to bed and fell asleep immediately. Early the next morning, her phone rang. It was the front desk manager. "Ma'am, someone will be there in the afternoon to do the repairs,"he promised.

She decided to order a light breakfast through room service, which they delivered very quickly. When she was finished, she placed the tray outside the front door. Then she made herself some tea.

"What a nice day!" Breezi thought. I should change out of my PJ's and take a look around, she decided. Breezi changed her clothes. She wore beige shorts, a blue top and kicked off her sandals, wanting to feel the cool sand between her toes.

The day before she didn't have a chance to see the grounds near her.. Breezi walked toward the curtained window that she had not opened.

A breathtaking sight appeared before her. She behold a private cove, with a rowboat, white sandy beach, chairs, coconuts and palm trees.

The turquoise water lapped onto the powdery beach. Under the palm trees were lounge chairs. The gentle winds called her name. Trees swayed. This exceeded her expectations, Breezi sighed and sat down taking in the view.

Time flew by as she slept in the lounge chair. Now early afternoon, she opted for lunch. Her stomach was growling again. She headed back to her bungalow.

A worker tapped lightly on her door. "Ma'am, hello?" the worker inquired. "I am here about the repairs," he reported.

"Just a minute, please," Breezi replied, she opened the door.

Breezi was startled to see the man in front of
her; he was so familiar, but carrying a tool bucket,

she couldn't place him. His strong tanned physique, blond hair and blue eyes were set off by yellow palm tree shirt with khaki shorts and sandals.

"Please come in. Sorry, I forgot my manners." Then it came to her.

"Were you on the same plane as me the other day? I thought I saw you there," she stammered.

"Yes, I thought you looked familiar! My name is Sande. I am working here for the summer. I know it's a little unusual, but I came out from the States as a favor for one of my clients whose relative owns the resort. They needed someone to help with hotel repair." He held out his hand. "Nice to meet you."

Breezi shook his hand firmly. "Thank you for coming out so quickly. I will let you get to the repairs, since they may take a while to complete. I'll be around, if you need anything." Breezi added. "There is a glass of water for you on the table."

It took a few hours. "Ma'am, I will have to come back later with a ladder to re-attach the roof fronds." Reappearing with the ladder Sande laid it against the roof near the hole.

He cautiously climbed up onto the roof. It was tricky attaching the fronds, while making sure he didn't fall through the holes. It was slow going.

"Thank you very much for all your help." Breezi replied. "But please call me Breezi, Sande, not Ma'am," she asked.

That night Breezi walked around her bungalow. She didn't want to miss anything that might need fixing. It was late so she lay down and went to sleep.

The next morning, she decided to call the front desk again, asking for Sande. "He was so helpful yesterday, can he please come out to bungalow 36 again, when he has a chance," Breezi inquired.

"I have another chore." she uttered. "Sure Ma'am, not a problem," the front desk clerk replied.

A few hours later her phone rang. "Hello?" Breezi answered. "Hello Ma'am, oh sorry, Breezi, this is Sande. I understand you have some more items that need to be looked at."

"Yes, thank you Sande, for responding so quickly," she replied. Please come by and fix the front door which squeaks and tighten up the hinges on the shutters." Breezi asked.

"Can you come by tomorrow? I might find some more items that need fixing," Breezi asked shyly.

"Sure," he said. "See you tomorrow."

Breezi began to like him very much. He was kind and gentle and his courteous demeanor impressed her. Sande felt good about fixing things. He was happy to return to the bungalow the next day as promised.

Sande followed her through the bungalow to the curtained door. "What a beautiful private view you have," he exclaimed. "I don't think other bungalows have this. You have your own cove, beach and boat. How amazing this is," Sande continued.

"Thank you, I love it," Breezi responded. "I have a question about the coconuts in the front and back palm trees . Would they come loose and fall on me if I sat in the lounge chair?" Breezi posed. She suggested they take a walk so she could show him the palms with the loose coconuts.

Sande was a good listener and told her that the coconuts wouldn't be a problem. Forming a friendship was a first for Sande in his new summer position working at a hotel.

"May I ask you another question? I might need help with the rowboat. Do you know where the life jackets are kept?" Breezi inquired.

"I can come by after work tomorrow and help you with that, if that is okay?" Sande asked.

"Sure," Breezi sighed. She felt a passionate attraction for Sande; yet she didn't want to appear too eager. These feelings were new for her.

While sleeping, she began to dream about Sande. That night a poem entered her dream. She named the poem My Heart.

My Heart

My love is as vast as the ocean.
I yearn to swim and dive
With the beating of my heart.
I reach through the ocean waves
to you.

She awoke in the middle of the night.. She couldn't sleep. She decided impulsively to pick up her phone. There was a big time difference where she lived in her apartment, but she had to talk with someone.

Timi heard the phone ring and picked it up and replied in a sleepy voice, "Hello?"

"Timi, guess what?" Breezi replied excitedly. At such a late hour it took Timi a few minutes to realize who was on the phone.

"Oh, Breezi! Are you ok? What's up?'

"Timi, I think I met someone on the island that I really like and I can't sleep." Timi was patient listener and was really happy for her friend. They talked for a while, Timi suddenly realized she had to go to work in a few hours. "Breezi, can we talk again when it's not midnight?"

"I'm so sorry!" Breezi replied forgetting how late she kept her friend up. She made a note to call her back another day.

Breezi's mind was active. Did Sande feel the same

attraction as she did? Her body was aching. She tossed and turned before finally falling asleep.

In fact, Sande was also anxious. He had a hard time sleeping too, because he found he was infatuated with Breezi and was feeling physically attracted to her.

Sande was feeling panicky and spontaneously called his parents for advice. "Dad, are you awake? I'm sorry it's late. I can't sleep. I think I met someone special." His dad mumbled, "Okay, let's talk."

"How did you know mom was the one for you?"

His dad started the conversation explaining that his family was in the farming business. They had always grown corn, raised chickens and cows. "I was always helping my parents at the fairs, showing the animals too.

"I was always shy," he admitted. "While at a local fair, your mom noticed me. She was looking at me and followed me. I was amused by her. Our eyes met whimsically. I was feeling nervous inside so it took me a few minutes to build up the courage to ask her out."

"After the first date, it was obvious that we both enjoyed each other very much. The relationship evolved as we learned about each other. The relationship grew into a bond of give and take. Soon after that we were married.

"Sande, it takes a lot of patience, love and respect for each other to make a marriage work," his father noted.

After a long conversation, Sande felt reassured after hearing his dad's advice. He thanked his dad .

The next day, Breezi woke up early and dressed quickly. She fixed breakfast and strolled down to the beach. She sat down on the lounge chair under the palm trees, looking forward to an easy, relaxing day.

Gentle breezes blew through her brown hair as she kicked off her sandals. Her legs were stretched and heels were dug in the soft sand. She closed her eyes and breathed slowly.

As she thought about Sande, Breezi's palms began to sweat and her heart began to flutter. Maybe she should ask him to stroll on the beach tomorrow? She hesitated. Maybe he had a full schedule after work?.

After lunch, Sande appeared at her bungalow, quickly rapping on the door frame.

"Hello? Ma'am, are you there?"

"Yes," Breezi replied, "Please come inside."

"The shutters look great and the roof held well during the breezes last night," Breezi told Sande.

"May I ask you a question? Please tell me if it is appropriate to ask." Breezi was afraid to ask him, she was nervous.

"Sande, would you like to walk on the beach tomorrow with me after work or on your day off." Breezi posed.

He looked around smiling at her. "Why not?" he beamed and waved as he walked down the path and informed her, "My schedule is pretty flexible right now."

Sande came by early. They both sat in the lounge chairs talking, laughing the day away. They quenched their thirst with the drinks they brought from her kitchen to the beach.

He explained that the green coconuts on the beach

had some refreshing coconut water inside of them once the tops were lopped off by a machete. A few feet away was a low bending palm tree with hanging coconuts which could be reached. He pulled one off and opened one. The juice was sweet and refreshing.

At the end of the day, he waved goodbye to her and said, "See you soon."

Breezi pushed open the sliding door to see another perfect day had arrived.

Sande arrived later in the day, and they began to splash themselves in the small wakes of the waves which gently rolled on the sand. Their clothes were damp from the water.

They were playfully chasing each other, flinging their flip flops and then running after them. They both stopped after a while, since they were out of breath and needed to sit down. They were both laughing.

Breezi was feeling very happy inside. Maybe this is the start of something great, she thought, while looking at the horizon.

At the same time, Sande was thinking the same thing as Breezi, as he glanced at her.

While they were staring at the horizon, Sande thought about things to say. Maybe I should ask if I can kiss her? he thought. Am I moving too fast? He was a little nervous.

"Would you mind if I held your hand?" Sande reached, over.

"Thanks for a great day," he sighed.

"You're welcome." Breezi murmured.

They both stood there looking at the sunset, its many colors flooding the sky, water lapping at their ankles, toes dug into the sand. Their flip flops were laying a few yards away.

The expansive horizon was turning from dusk to sunset. Breezi's hair glistened with golden streaks from the sun's fading rays of sunlight.

Things were changing so quickly for her.

"Maybe we can use the rowboat tomorrow? What do you think, Sande?" Breezi invited.

"Sure," he rejoined. He was smiling too. He said, "Goodbye, see you tomorrow around noon!" as he walked down the path.

Breezi went back to the cottage and packed a few sandwiches put them in the fridge. The water bottles were filled. During the night she tossed and turned from excitement.

The next morning Sande walked briskly up the

driveway with some extra water bottles, wearing his favorite hat and sunglasses. He was thinking ahead eagerly and wondering if he would have the nerve to ask Breezi for a kiss.

It was such a beautiful day with a warm, blowing breeze. Gentle waves lapped at the boat's hull. Breezi wore her hat and light clothing, grabbed the sandwich cooler, and a life jackets.

"Let me show you your island by boat," he exclaimed. "I can tell you about the town, the hotel's history, and how it came to be. That was part of my job training before I arrived here," Sande related to Breezi. Sande had spent hours researching online his job requirements and also found out about the island's interesting history.

"Are you ready for our next adventure?" invited Sande.

"Yes, many thanks." Breezi giggled.,grabbing the sides of the boat, climbed in. She put on the life jacket, sitting down excitedly. She handed Sande his jacket as he sat down.

The boat rocked rhythmically on the water. Breezi untied the rope from the wooden post near the shore.

Sande took the oars and began to row gently. The oars moved the boat slowly, as it cruised it on the cove.

Just think, Breezi thought, my own private island cove! It was starting to seem like things were magically falling in place for her.

Sande finally got the courage to ask Breezi a question. Looking into her eyes, the words came out of his mouth very slowly. "Am I moving too fast by going out with you today?" he asked.

Breezi looked at him, leaned over and started to kiss him passionately. This caught Sande by surprise at first. He found himself reciprocating, nearly dropped the oars in the water. Emotions hit them like a tidal wave!

They had to make sure they didn't capsize the boat while entwined in a long embrace. When they had recovered, Sande continued to row in the cove.

Sande explained the island's history, and the town when it was first settled. He was trying to concentrate as he was rowing. Breezi listened intently.

Time passed by slowly and soon they both began to feel hungry. Breezi pulled out the sandwiches she made from the bungalow's kitchen and gave one to Sande. He took a few sips from the bottled water.

"Are you tired?" Breezi asked. "I can try to take over, you just have to show me how to row the boat."

"I'll keep rowing, but I'd happily show you how to row later today or another day. Thank you for asking, but I can handle it now," Sande assured Breezi.

"Sande, Breezi mentioned, we've been on the water for several hours, do you think we should be turning back?" she questioned. Grabbing the oars Sande tried to turn the boat around heading towards shore.

"Maybe we'll go swimming tomorrow in the shallow part." Breezi suggested. She didn't realize how deep the cove was, glancing over the side nervously. She had forgotten that she didn't know how to swim well.

Little did they know they were drifting along on an ocean current. They went further and further away from the shore towards the ocean waves. The undertow became stronger and stronger pulling them away from the gentle cove.

Sande was struggling for a while trying to turn them back towards the bungalows. Late day distant storm clouds crept quickly upon them. The sky turned dark and ominous.

Suddenly the wind started to pick up, the water became very choppy. They didn't know what to do. Large raindrops pelted hard on them, the rowboat started rocking to and fro. The winds became fierce.

Breezi started to panic. The waves had crests on them. Sande tried to keep the boat afloat . Visibility was very poor. The waves were huge. They spied a large gray object in the water a few hundred feet away

"Maybe if we reach that, it will be safer than in the open water, she remarked pointing to something, It looks like an island." shouted Breezi above the howling winds. Sande was pulling hard with all his might and rowed towards it. His hands were sore, red and his muscles ached.

Just as they approached the grey object, it blew a stream of water from the top of its spout. "Oh!" Sande shouted." It's a whale!" Breezi's body started to shake and she began to pray aloud. "Please bring us home safe. Protect us from the whale's fluke and tail," she expressed. Breezi remembered from her school lessons a story about a whale, but had never seen a real one.

The female whale was floating around. It seemed to be in distress, noted Sande. Breezi's body trembled fiercely. Her queasy stomach tested her.

They noticed some fishing line wrapped around one part of the fluke. Maybe it was in trouble. The clouds in the sky changed slowly. The winds calmed down.

The rain stopped, the waves died down, yet they were still so huge for Breezi.

The whale's fluke was so near the boat, she felt like she could almost touch it. She had to focus on her breathing, in and out, nice and slow, to calm herself. Breezi didn't know how to swim. She was overwhelmed with fear, but she felt awed by being so close to the whale.

What if the whale panicked and they were capsized and drowned? Breezi shook in terror.

Sande found a knife in the first aid kit and decided to try to help the whale. He took some deep breaths, leaving his fate to the ocean.

Diving over the side, he was able to slowly untangle the line, by carefully cutting it away. After coming up frequently for air, he succeeded in freeing the whale.

Breezi was sitting in the boat all alone, holding on for dear life, making sure the rowboat didn't tip. Her hands hurt, her knuckles had turned white. It took all her strength to keep the oars in the boat. Her stomach was in a knot.

The whale looked at Breezi, and seemed to understand that they were trying to help her. It didn't move, just floated in the ocean.

The rescue seemed to take forever. Sande finally broke the surface of the waves. Breezi was relieved that Sande was still alive and didn't drown or suffer injury. She began to feel better.

Sande removed all the line off the fluke and dragged it into the boat with Breezi's assistance.

Breezi suddenly got a crazy idea. "What would happen if we wrapped a tow rope to the whale's fluke and it could pull us home," she offered. They pondered this idea. The whale seemed to understand that they needed help and didn't swim away.

They talked out loud with each other, asking the angels for help and guidance. Their prayers were answered! Gently the whale took the tow rope and pulled them towards the cove.

When Sande and Breezi got their bearings they thanked the whale and hated to let her go. Way out on the horizon the whale jumped an amazing high breech out of the water before swimming away, as a thank you.

Reality hit them both realizing how huge the blue whale was. When they were freeing her the dark water hid her body length well.

When Breezi was finally breathing normally, she said in a joking tone, "I didn't mean I wanted to swim in the ocean, when I said that earlier. I only wanted to learn how to swim in the cove."

The sun had started to descend. Twilight was approaching and Breezi was worried that they wouldn't make it to shore before dark.

Sande was exhausted, his hands were blistered. They weren't going to make it back to the bungalow before dark. He couldn't row anymore.

They might have to sleep in the boat on the cove, with only a small anchor to put in the water he thought.

Sande coached Breezi on how to take over the oars. It took a long time because Breezi didn't know how to coordinate her arms and muscles at first. It took a little while until she understood.

The twinkling lights of the nearby bungalows dotted the shores. The palms gently swayed to and fro as the setting sun cooled the warm breezes.

There was just enough light to see before the setting sun disappeared With her last bit of energy, Breezi rowed towards a distant shoreline where they could pull the boat ashore. Many of the bungalows looked all the same at night.

Since she had grown up in a small village, she knew how to build a fire and make shelter with some fronds she found. She also knew how to catch a fish for dinner. As a child occasionally she would catch fish from fishing in the local creek.

They used the last crumbs of their lunch as bait to catch a fish in the shallow water. They gutted and cooked it for dinner over the open flame using the knife from the safety kit. They used a stick to cook it. They used stones to set a ring that contained the fire. The had to eat quickly since the fire was beginning to die out. Now they were in total darkness.

During the night little ghost crabs swam from the bottom of the ocean waves. They scurried to and fro onto the beach sand looking for food in the sands before returning to the water.

A chill filled the air. They huddled together to keep warm. Their bodies were sore and worn out. She felt a little scared about how close she was to Sande. They finally fell asleep lulled by the rhythms of the ocean waves and twinkling of the stars.

The moon served as their nightlight. They slept in the sand. Their hair plastered with the salt water and sand. The sticky skin on their bodies itched,.

Like the strong undertow of the ocean waves, Breezi and Sande were meshed together physically and emotionally from the beginning of their adventure. The night sky turned different colors. A large sun was beginning to rise. It was a new day.

They stretched and rose up from their challenged sleep. Birds began to chirp.

Their prayers had been answered! They weren't too far away from Breezi's bungalow. It was sheer luck!

They quickly stripped off their clothes on the way to the outdoor shower. Both of them felt excitement and magnetic pull to each other. They started moaning as they pressed their fiery bodies together.

Breezi felt lust and desire like she had never known before. Their bodies were intense and wet.

Sande passionately pushed her up against the shower wall with his arms. Breezi surrendered fully to his strength. Her knees were weak and she could feel Sande's strength holding her up.

They merged together caressing and kissing each other as soothing waters flowed down their bodies. There was a wild abandoning of everything they knew. There was a natural and free feeling, like the ebb and flow of the ocean waters. They were like two pieces of a puzzle joining together as one.

Afterwards they picked up their clothes and freely sat naked on the lounge chairs. They laughed and were amazed by their connection, reading each other's thoughts.

With renewed energy they rushed into the bungalow bedroom, leaving their clothes strewn everywhere. They connected sexually and sensually all day.

These two lovers were sweaty and exhausted. They flopped down on the pillows, curled up and fell asleep.

Around dawn the next morning, Sande rose and took a shower. Gently kissing Breezi, he said "Good morning my love. I'll see you later. I've got to go to work." Wearing his work clothes he ran out the door.

Breezi mumbled something and went back to sleep. Realizing last night was not a dream, she glided her hand to the warm place where Sande had been lying.

Eventually, dreamily Breezi awakened, took a shower, and dressed. She made breakfast. When she was finished she strolled to the beach. Glowing from last night's doings and the intensity of the relationship, Breezi feared the time flying by.

She began to panic. This amazing feeling was new to her and yet she feared it might end soon. She would be leaving and flying home to the mainland, leaving him and the relationship behind. What was she going to do?

The hotel management saw a great deal of potential in Sande after his being there a short time. They appreciated the quality of his work. Even with his taking time off to be with Breezi, he had worked long days. Sande felt apprehensive about time moving quickly, as this was a summer position.

The workload kept him busy. Finally Sande found time to ride into town. He wanted to look around and familiarize himself with some of the local shops.

He hadn't had a chance to meet the locals who ran the town: the shopkeepers, policemen, librarian and other merchants.

Sande introduced himself to a friendly police officer, who doubled as the local clergyman. He felt comfortable knowing there was someone he could turn to if there were any problems with a guest at the hotel. Looking to his right he found a small pawn shop. He walked in.

People must have been in financial trouble he thought, looking around. They have a lot of nice items. Then his eyes spied something in a glass case, stopping him in his tracks.

His relationship new with Breezi, Sande didn't have time to think about next steps.

A nice ring had been used for collateral to receive money, he assumed. It sat by itself. Sande took a guess not knowing Breezi's ring size. It was perfect. Simple but elegant. He paid for it. It was spontaneous and yet it felt right.

Whistling Sande picked it up, jumped into the jeep. Sande knew he had a meeting that night. Sande put the ring away in his room. He felt unsure about what their future held, because it was unfolding so quickly.

He reflected on how he had met the policeman earlier that day, who also happened to be the town clergyman. Everything seemed to be happening effortlessly, and yet, it still felt a little scary.

The management called him into the office the next night. He didn't know what to think. They talked about rearranging duties and schedules with the staff.

He was a bundle of nerves, his stomach was doing flips.Sande put on his best face and marched up to the office, not sure what was going to happen. He thought, "I am going to be laid off the job because it was only a temporary position? What will I tell Breezi? What is next for us?" His heart sank.

"Sande, welcome, come in please." The manager shook his hand, showing him the chair to sit down. "We are very pleased with your work here," he complimented. After a few minutes he went on to ask Sande if he would like to stay on with a permanent position as assistant manager.

Sande was stunned, his jaw dropping open. "T-t-th-h-ank you very much, sir," he stammered. "I thought I was being terminated since it was a temporary position for the summer." Sande added.

"That is ridiculous," chuckled his boss. "Please think about it and give me an answer in a few days," he offered.

Sande walked about the grounds for a long time, just thinking. He had to think about both his job and his newly developing future with Breezi.

He decided to go back to his manager and ask him a question. "I wanted to ask if you are hiring any other positions, for other people," he continued. Sande wasn't comfortable yet, sharing his ideas about possibly working with Breezi here on the island. "Sure," his boss revealed.

"You would choose your hours and who you wanted to hire to work with you, etc." Sande's boss continued.

"Ok thanks. I will give you an answer soon," Sande promised turning to go.

It was very late when Sande strolled into the bungalow. He had a serious look on his face and sat down. "I want to ask you a few questions Breezi," he said.

Breezi had been crying. She was thinking that something bad must have happened. He was away so long. Tears running down her face, sobbing uncontrollably, her face in her hands. Her chin quivered.

"I'm so sorry you were sacked. What are you going to do?" Breezi presented. "What are we going to do?"

"Whoa, wait a minute, what is all this, love?" Sande exclaimed rushing over to her side.

Sande held Breezi in his arms, stroked her hair and dried her tears. Breezi babbled, fearing their relationship was going to end soon. "Will you be leaving? I'm scared, I know my vacation is ending soon. I may never see you again!" Breezi's eyes refilling with tears.

Sande was quiet, he helped her calm down. "I have something to tell you." he whispered.

"Where I used to live, there were no real jobs that I could find after I graduated. I was going to move to another city and this opportunity came my way," Sande told Breezi.

"Breezi, I am so happy being with you. You've changed my life. I want to ask you something important," Sande answered. "How much do you like this place? Would you consider living here permanently with me?"

Breezi was puzzled and confused. "Wait, didn't they sack you?"she persisted.

"No, They offered me a permanent position as assistant manager!" he exclaimed. "They said the job has flexible hours. There are other positions available too, and I need to give them an answer very soon," Sande related.

Breezi, sunk down in the chair, shocked and overjoyed for both of them. She never thought about moving to an island for her home. This was so new to her, finding love, and feeling happiness so quickly.

Breezi reflected on the move, her job. The people were so friendly and kind here. This would be an ideal, dream place to live. There was so much to do here. The weather was warm and the island wasn't far from the mainland. She could fly and visit friends and family. The flights weren't very long. Everything seemed perfect.

Breezi had her back turned away from Sande. She was facing the sliding door, watching the beach waves crashing on the shore.

Her emotions flipped and flopped! Shock from the rapid changes and overjoyed by all the exciting possibilities intrigued her.

Her heart rose in her throat and her legs shook. She felt physically drained and holding onto a chair for support. Very slowly Breezi turned around.

Sande had dropped on one knee holding out the ring that he'd purchased.

"Breezi, will you marry me? Be my wife?" he stammered.

Breezi shrieked with delight. Her hand flew up to her mouth. "Yes! Yes, Yes I will!" She began jumping up and down excitedly, flinging her arms around him.

"If this a dream, please don't wake me up!" She yelled grabbing his face, kissing him all over. Her hand was shaking while he put the ring on Breezi's finger. It fit well!

Breezi had agreed to become his wife. Sande cried happy tears that night as they ran into the bedroom, turning out the light.

In the morning, Sande asked Breezi if she could imagine a suitable position for her, working at the resort.

"Of course" she answered. With a big smile on his face, he phoned his boss to tell him the good news that both he and Breezi would be staying and working there.

Breezi phoned her parents early, crying. Breezi's mother panicked, "What is wrong? Bree," her concern obvious.

"Mum, I'm just so happy." she sniffed. "I found my true love and although it seems incredibly sudden, I'm getting married to a wonderful man named Sande! He proposed to me last night. Sande was promoted to assistant manager yesterday and we're going to live on this vacation island that I've been telling you about."

"That is wonderful Bree! Wait until I tell your father!" Breezi's mother, Sara, was crying now too.

"Now your father has no excuse not to travel to

visit you. Let me help you with the wedding plans! I am so excited for you."

Breezi's father was talking in the background. "Hold on, John. Guess what? Our baby girl's getting married."

"Can I talk to her too,?" John asked.

"Sure, give me a moment love. Ok?" Sara pleaded. Breezi, can you put your fiancé on the phone, please?"

"Sure. Sande, my mother and father want to talk to you." Sande rolled his eyes nervously, swallowing hard. Breezi handed the phone to him.

"Oh, boy, what should I call her?" he mouthed to Breezi.

"What is her name, Sara? Your father's name is John, right?" Breezi nodded.

Sande took a big breath, slowly "How about first start by saying hello?" Breezi chuckled.

"Hello, Breeezi's mother." Sande spoke very softly.

"Welcome to the family, Sande," Sara replied. "Please call me Sara. I look forward to meeting you soon. So does my husband John. Thank you for loving our daughter by showing her respect, kindness and allowing her to be herself. It takes a wonderful man with a big heart to love this much," Sara instructed.

"Sara, thank you for bringing up a wonderful daughter with good values," Sande smiled. "Can I speak with your husband a little later today?" he ventured.

"Of course, goodbye for now," Sande replied hanging up the phone.

"Whew! Sande sighed. " I wasn't sure what to say to your parents." Sande told Breezi.

His next call would be to his parents. They had never traveled outside the United States. That would be a great adventure for them to meet Breezi's parents in East Africa and be part of the planning.

Sande dialed their number in the United States. There was a lot of interference on the line. "Mom, I'm getting married!" he shouted.

"What? Who is this?" Cindy inquired. "Oh, Sande!"

"Wait a minute son, I can't hear you. It's too loud," his mom replied. There was a lot of clucking and squawking in the background. "Who's getting married?" Cindy replied. "Me and Breezi!" Sande spoke loudly. "I asked her last night and she said yes!"

"That is wonderful, congratulations!" I knew she was the one when you first told your father about her. Frank, Sande is getting married to Breezi!" Sande's mom communicated.

"He picked a wonderful person" Frank replied. "Didn't they see each other on the same plane going to the island resort? It sure unfolding magically for them," remembered Frank.

"Now we can go on vacation too and visit her parents in East Africa," Cindy volunteered.

Breezi was so happy. Her heart was full and she was floating on cloud nine. She had been exchanging texts with her parents and her friend Timi since the beginning of the vacation. Timi explained that the workload was crazy since she left. Breezi texted her back, "Sorry, feeling a little guilty here."

Sande was a dream come true for her, she couldn't believe what was happening between them. Her entire future was changing. The last phone calls Breezi had to make were to her boss and then to her best friend, Timi, who gave her this opportunity to go on this vacation. Breezi asked Timi if she would be the bridesmaid.

"Of course," Timi exclaimed. "I will come out there and we can talk about the wedding plans. I'm so happy for you both. Let's talk soon."

This was a new adventure for all of them. Breezi flew back to the mainland with Sande. Timi had arranged a going away shower with Breezi's former co-workers for her and Sande.

They all had a great time. When that was over, they visited both parents for a short visit and Breezi decided to buy her dress while she was visiting her parents instead of getting it shipped to the island.

The future bride and groom decided to include some cultural tradition from both of their countries into the wedding. Breezi chose some of her favorite Kenyan music that she grew up with. Sande incorporated his favorite country music.

Both parents came out to visit and help with the plans, along with Timi.

"I am so happy to be your bridesmaid." Timi exclaimed.

Sande asked his boss to be his best man. "Are you sure?"he asked. "I am so honored, and as my gift to you I will provide the food for everyone for the reception."

Sande contacted the clergyman earlier in the year making sure he was available to officiate at their wedding. Wedding email invitations were sent out to the guests.

The wedding rehearsal was taking place after many weeks of planning. Tables and chairs filled the area near their bungalow. The tables were decorated with beautifully colored flowers and lovely place settings. Two rows of coconuts lined the aisle from the bungalow to the sandy beach where the ceremony was to take place.It was easier than purchasing a runner for a walkway.

After the rehearsal, everyone gathered on the

beach. They had all heard the whale adventure. They thought it was just an exaggerated story.

Far out in the ocean, a female blue whale had swum near the cove entrance. She seemed to be waiting for something. The couple had turned to the horizon one last time with everyone looking.

"Look our whale!" they both shouted and pointed her out to the group. She was spouting a huge fountain of water from her blow hole as a send-off, before swimming away. She was saying goodbye to us. Now everyone had seen her.

They all stayed up late, sitting around a campfire on the beach. Suddenly the guests realized they had to head to bed - they had to prepare for the wedding the next day. Guests walked to different bungalows for the night. Breezi's parents walked to her bungalow, Sande walked to his parents.

The wedding day arrived. The morning sun had risen over the horizon. Everyone was eating breakfast in his bungalow. Time flew by quickly on this lovely day. Palm branches swayed in the gentle breeze. Rustling of leaves continued. The time for the ceremony to begin arrived.

Softly, the beat of the background music played, before Breezi came out. Sande stood at the assigned spot waiting patiently for Breezi. Breezie carrying her bouquet emerged on the sandy beach.

A lone African drum beat softly in perfect rhythm as Breezi walked on the sand to meet Sande. He felt the tears falling from his eyes as he watched his bride walking towards him. He had never seen her so beautiful.

When Breezi stopped, Timi stood with her cell phone playing the wedding march through a few tiny speakers.

The clergyman asked who was giving them away. Both parents stood up from their stools and declared that they were both giving away their children at the same time. The parents held each other up so they wouldn't fall from shaking.

Breezi wore a yellow chiffon tea length dress with sandals. On her wrists she wore African bracelets, her hair was styled high on her head. She was so excited her body was shaking. Timi held her bouquet and stood next to the clergyman.

Sande wore an African shirt and khaki pants and stood barefoot. They were both very creative. The ceremony had some music from both of their American and African cultures along with the vows they had written themselves.

The ceremony was being held on the beach where they had met behind her bungalow. They were surrounded by family and friends. It was late morning on the first day of spring. There wasn't a dry eye throughout the whole wedding.

The clergyman cleared his throat after their vows were spoken by saying, "By the power vested in me, I now pronounce you husband and wife. You may kiss your bride." Everyone cheered.

When the ceremony concluded everyone sat at tables where the food was laid out colorfully and plentifully. Guests were offered mango drinks and local Kenyan beer for starters. Fresh tropical fruits were then served including pineapple, paw-paw, guava, and avocado.

Delicious entree choices included beef stew, chicken, and fish. For side dishes there was African porridge, maize and beans, potatoes and assorted vegetables.

After eating, music played in the background for dancing. The sun began to set. The tiki torches were lit and burning, bringing firelight to the bungalow and the beach. After many hours, the exhausted guests retired to their bungalows.

The newly wedded couple were alone on the beach sitting in their lounge chairs.

Sande and Breezi held champagne glasses while their other hands grasped each other. They were staring into each other's eyes. Their souls were as one. The light from the moon cast a long shadow from them on the sandy beach.

Early the next morning after saying goodbye to the newlyweds, the guests drove to the airport to board planes back to the mainland.

Sande and Breezi magically encountered one

another on this special journey. This was the beginning of hundreds of magnificent experiences that would unfold during their long sweet, loving marriage.

www.ingramcontent.com/pod-product-compliance
Lightning Source LLC
Chambersburg PA
CBHW040742250626
47164CB00001BA/9